Sam's

USA
20

CONTENTS

CHAPTER 1
WISHFUL THINKING

Sam's dad is a courier driver.
Every morning, he takes Sam
to school, then he drives off
in his van to pick up and deliver
parcels and mail.

Sam thinks her dad's job
is boring.

Sam wishes her dad had an exciting job like Jessica's dad. He is an archaeologist. He digs for ancient bones, tools, and pottery. He sends Jessica postcards from Central America and Mexico.

Guatemala

March 16
Mayan Excavations,
Tikal, Guatemala

Dear Jessica,
Today I dug up
a Mayan axe blade.
It's made of shiny, black
volcanic glass known as
obsidian. It's very hot digging in this jungle.

Love Dad

GUATEMALA
3-16

GUATEMALA
Correo aéreo
Q. 3.00

Jessica Morris
251 Maple Avenue,
Eagle Rock,
CA 90263,
U.S.A.

Sam wishes her dad had a job like Tom's mum. Tom's mum is a pilot. She flies planes all over the world. She sends faxes, e-mails, and postcards to Tom from fun and fascinating places.

HOTEL LANTAU

Date: March 20
Fax From: Diana Farrant
                Hong Kong
Fax To: Tom Farrant

Hello, Tom
There are nearly seven million
people living in Hong Kong.
No wonder it's so noisy.
It's easier to land the 747s
at the new airport on
Lantau Island. Thank goodness!

Love Mum
PS I hope you're working hard
at school.

On Sam's classroom wall,
there is a world map. There are
red pins and blue pins scattered
all over it.

Miss Perez put a red pin
in Central America to show
where Jessica's dad was.
She put a blue pin in Hong Kong
to show where Tom's mum was.

"Your parents are teaching
us geography by mail,"
Miss Perez said to Jessica
and Tom.

Sam wished her dad could
teach geography, too.

One day, Jessica brought to school a postcard from Guatemala.

Guatemala

March 29
Mayan Excavations,
Tikal, Guatemala

GUATEMALA
3-29

GUATEMALA
Correo aéreo
Q. 3.00

Hi, Jessica
Today I dug up a skull.
It has blue beads in its
mouth. These were used to
buy things in the next world.
We're excited because only
the kings and queens had them.

Jessica Morris
251 Maple Avenue,
Eagle Rock,
CA 90263,
U.S.A.

Love Dad
PS Did you get the blue plastic beads I sent?

Tom's mum had sent him
a postcard from France.

March 28
Paris, France

Bonjour, Tom

I was going to
send a fax, but I
thought you might
like a postcard
from Paris for
your scrapbook.

After breakfast
(le petit déjeuner),
we're going to
climb the Eiffel
Tower. It's 300
metres high.

Love Mum

Tom Farrant
156 Birch Drive,
Eagle Rock,
CA 90263, U.S.A.

14

"Look, I'm a queen,"
said Jessica, wearing the blue
plastic beads her dad had sent her.

"A fax is faster," said Tom,
"but I really like the coloured
pictures on a postcard better."

He put a blue pin on
Paris, France.

Sam said nothing.

A week later, they read Jessica's postcard from Honduras.

16

HONDURAS

14 LEMPIRAS   CORREO AÉREO

HONDURAS

April 7
Mayan Excavations,
Copán,
Honduras

Jessica Morris
251 Maple Avenue,
Eagle Rock,
CA 90263,
U.S.A.

Dear Jessica,
The ancient
Mayans used
sculpture to
record important
dates and events in their rulers' lives.
Mail was sent by runners.
When one got tired, he gave
the message to someone else —
a bit slow!

I will be going to Yucatán,
Mexico, soon.

Love Dad

Then Miss Perez put a blue pin
in the map, and the class
gathered around the computer.
Tom's mum had sent him
an e-mail on the Internet
from New York.

From: **Diana Farrant**

Sent: Tuesday, April 11, 2000, 7:00 A.M.

To: Tom Farrant

Subject: **Hello from New York**

Dear Tom and Friends,

This is an easy way to send
a letter. I don't have to find
a stamp, or even a post office.
It's just as well, because the airport
in New York is as big as a city.
It's easy to get lost. Hundreds of
planes from all over the world land
here every day. I hope you're
all enjoying school.

Love from Tom's mum

Then Sam got some mail, too. She had a postcard from Arizona. Her dad had posted it when he went there to deliver some parcels.

Miss Perez smiled at Sam and gave her a yellow pin to put in the map. Sam thought it wasn't quite the same as mail from other countries. She wished her dad went to more exciting places.

April 13

Howdy, Sam

The picture on the front
shows what it's like here
in Arizona — dry land
as far as the eye can see.

Love Dad
PS See you
tomorrow after school.

Sam Webb
52 Pine Grove,
Eagle Rock,
CA 90263

ARIZONA

CHAPTER 3
SPORTS DAY

The following day, Miss Perez said, "Next month is our sports day with other schools. Today you're going to write letters to your parents, asking for helpers."

April 18
Mayan Excavations,
Yucatán, Mexico

Newtown School
Cherry Drive,
Eagle Rock,
CA 90263,
U.S.A.

Hi, Dad

We're having a school sports day next month. We need lots of helpers. Can you help?

Love Jessica

Jessica was sad when she
showed the class her next postcard.

24

Mexico

April 25
Mayan Excavations,
Yucatán, Mexico

4.60 pesos

MEXICO

Dear Jessica,
Sorry, I can't help
at school. I'll still be digging
up Mayan treasures. They're
going to be on display in the
museum. Isn't that exciting?

Love Dad

Jessica Morris

251 Maple Avenue,

Eagle Rock,

CA 90263,

U.S.A.

Tom was quiet as he read his latest e-mail and stuck a blue pin in Hawaii.

Hello from Hawaii – Microsoft Exchange

From: **Diana Farrant**

Sent: Thursday, April 27, 2000, 9:17 A.M.

To: Tom Farrant

Subject: **Hello from Hawaii**

Aloha, Tom

Sorry, I can't make it to help with the sports day. Just play hard but fair. Good luck.

It's warm and sunny here. I've scanned in a photo of the view from my hotel.

Love Mum

HAWAII.jpg

But Sam smiled as she waved
a letter in the air and put
a yellow pin in the map.

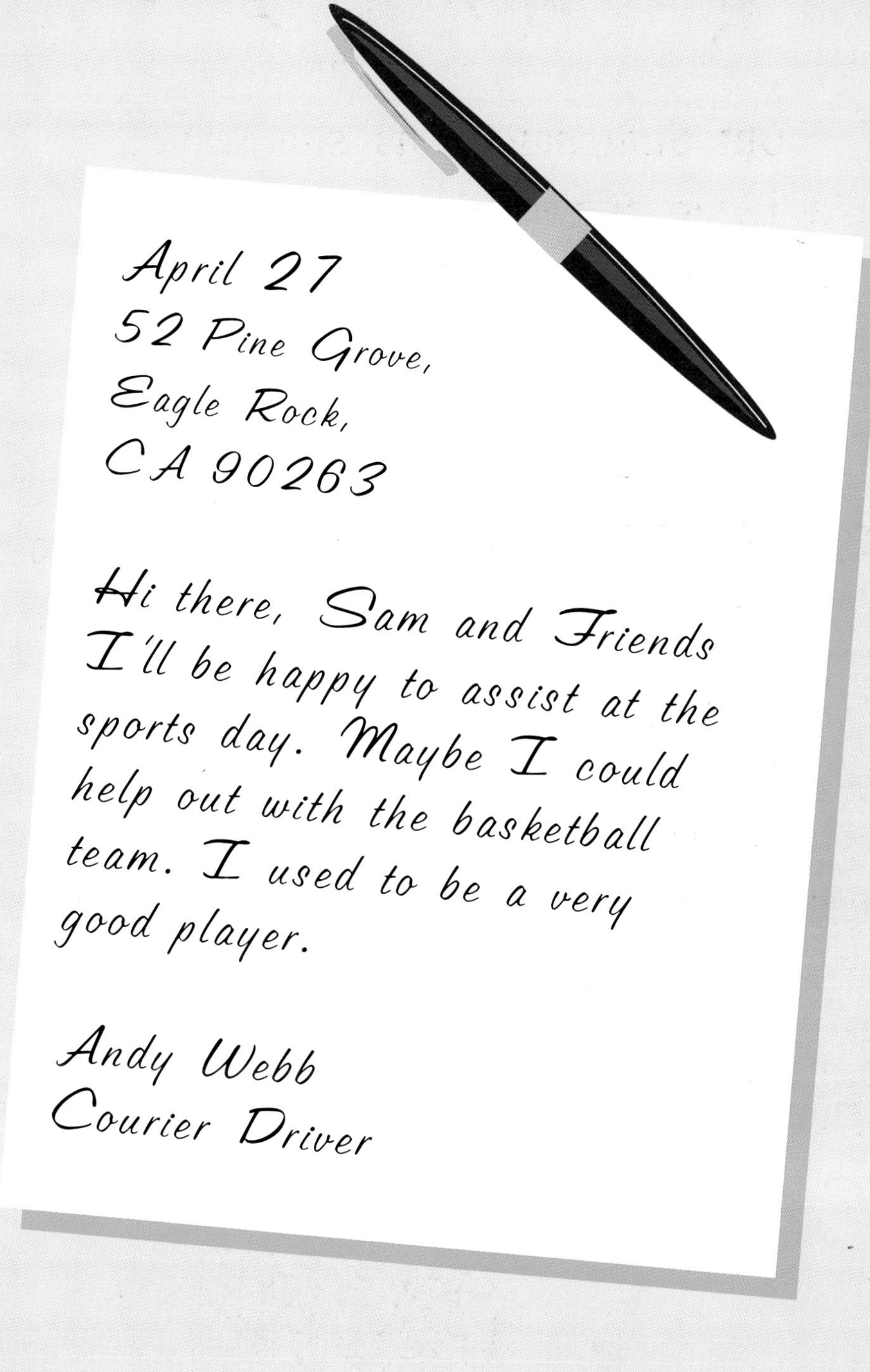

April 27
52 Pine Grove,
Eagle Rock,
CA 90263

Hi there, Sam and Friends
I'll be happy to assist at the
sports day. Maybe I could
help out with the basketball
team. I used to be a very
good player.

Andy Webb
Courier Driver

Suddenly, Sam knew she really did have a special dad after all.

What's more, without people like her dad, no one would get postcards and parcels from fun and fascinating places!

FROM THE AUTHOR

I overheard some children talking about their parents. They were all so proud of them in different ways. As I love getting mail, I decided to use all kinds of mail to tell this story. Perhaps you could send me some and tell me what you think of it.

Linley Jones

FROM THE ILLUSTRATOR

I related well to the father in this story. I work from home illustrating children's books, so I'm able to go to my children's sports days, as well as other events they may have. I also get to be one of the teachers at my children's annual winter art school.

Kelvin Hawley